STICKY ICKY VICKY

Courage over Fear

By Alysia & Michael Ssentamu

Illustrated by Noor Alshalabi

First published in 2021 by Pixel Publishing House

Cover, interior design and illustrations by Noor Alshalabi

ISBN 978-0-6451293-0-4 (paperback)
ISBN 978-0-6451293-1-1 (ebook)
ISBN 978-0-6451293-2-8 (audiobook)

For more information about the authors, illustrator, book and for some amazing free resources please head to: www.stickyickyvicky.com

Publisher's Cataloging-in-Publication Data
provided by Five Rainbows Cataloging Services

Names: Ssentamu, Alysia, author. | Ssentamu, Michael, author. | Alshalabi, Noor Mohammad, illustrator.

Title: Sticky icky Vicky : courage over fear / by Alysia Ssentamu [and] Michael Ssentamu ; Noor Mohammad Alshalabi, illustrator.

Description: Mawson, AU : Pixel Publishing House, 2021. | Series: Sticky icky Vicky. | Summary: Sticky Icky Vicky: Courage over Fear inspires children to overcome their own fears, through positivity and perseverance. | Audience: Ages 6-10.

Identifiers: ISBN 978-0-6451293-0-4 (paperback) | ISBN 978-0-6451293-1-1 (ebook) | | ISBN 978-0-6451293-2-8 (audiobook)

Subjects: LCSH: Children's stories. | CYAC: Fear--Fiction. | Self-confidence--Fiction. | Self-actualization (Psychology)--Fiction. | Girl--Fiction. | BISAC: JUVENILE FICTION / Social Themes / Self-Esteem & Self-Reliance. | JUVENILE FICTION / Social Themes / Values & Virtues. JUVENILE FICTION / Social Themes / Emotions & Feelings

Classification: LCC PZ7.1.S84 St 2021 (print) | LCC PZ7.1.S84 (ebook) | DDC [Fic]--dc23.

This book was inspired by our children. Never stop challenging us, asking questions and amazing us with your ability to learn and grow.

TO ALL MY READERS, I hope you enjoy this book and that you find the courage to overcome any fears you may have, like I did. Love from Sticky Icky Vicky.

VICKY is a charming, playful, outdoor-loving girl
with dark brown eyes and long hair with a curl.
She lives with her parents on Crescent Moon beach.
With blue waters stretching as far as the eye can reach.

Vicky likes to play at the playground with best friends Rhea and Betty.
Playing tips, swinging from monkey bars, and getting all sweaty.

She is often covered with dirt, looking all icky and sticky.

This is why her friends call her **STICKY ICKY VICKY**.

Vicky adores her nickname, wearing her dirt-covered clothes with pride.

Dirt gathered from dancing through mud and rolling down the dusty hillside.

All this messy fun is fine, if at the end of each day's play,

Vicky would get in the bath, but no, this is not her way.

Vicky has a fear of water and will bathe no more than once a week.

Only ever a brief shower, accompanied by a loud shriek.

"You can't always go around being icky and sticky," Vicky's mum says.

"It is nice to have a bath and get clean, especially after dirt play days."

"Not tonight Mum," replies Vicky. "It's cold and I am already in bed.

Let's read my favourite book and have a really long cuddle instead!"

THE LITTLE PRINCESS THAT COULD

Vicky's excuses and fear of water started after the accident by the sea.

She remembers it very clearly, even though she was only three.

Vicky was in the water, jumping waves, having lots of fun.

Next thing, she heard her mum shout, "RUN, VICKY, RUN!"

Just then a rogue wave hit, dragging Vicky out, spinning her round.

If not for her dad who saved her, Vicky would have drowned!

Vicky's fear of water sparks a voice in her head.

She calls this unhelpful inner voice, Negative Ned.

Negative Ned tells Vicky that she is not good enough.

"Don't go in the water," he says, "you are not brave or tough."

He reminds her of the fear she felt as the wave swept her out to sea.

This is why Sticky Icky Vicky has avoided water since the age of three.

One day while collecting shells on the beach in the early morning sun,
Vicky spots Rhea and Betty, swimming in the water, having lots of fun.

She thinks it would be nice to join them, but feels too scared and sheds a tear.
To go in the water with her friends someday, Vicky must choose courage over fear.

That afternoon, tired and hungry from building sandcastles at the beach, Sticky Icky Vicky and her friends sit down to share a peach.

After their snack, Betty gives Vicky a birthday invitation.
To Splash-tastic, the world's best water park destination.

YOU ARE INVITED TO

Betty's waterslide birthday bash.

Flip and Flop on over to celebrate her
8th birthday with a splash!

Vicky thinks of all the fun she will have with her friends at Splash-tastic.
Hurtling down waterslides with Rhea and Betty will be so FANTASTIC.

She decides she has missed out for too long and accepts Betty's invitation.

Trying to scare her, Negative Ned whispers, "Did you see the party's location?"

"Yes," Vicky replies, "but I'm not going to avoid water parks anymore."

"Water is dangerous," says Ned, "and you have not been to a water park before."

Vicky knows this, but decides the time is right for her to face her fear.

She'll go to the local pool the next morning, her goal and purpose are clear.

"How do you feel?" asks Vicky's dad, on their way to the pool the next day.
"Remember, Rhea and Betty will be there to support you every step of the way."
Vicky feels too anxious to answer, her heart hammering fast in her chest.
She knows this is not going to be easy, but she is ready to do her BEST.

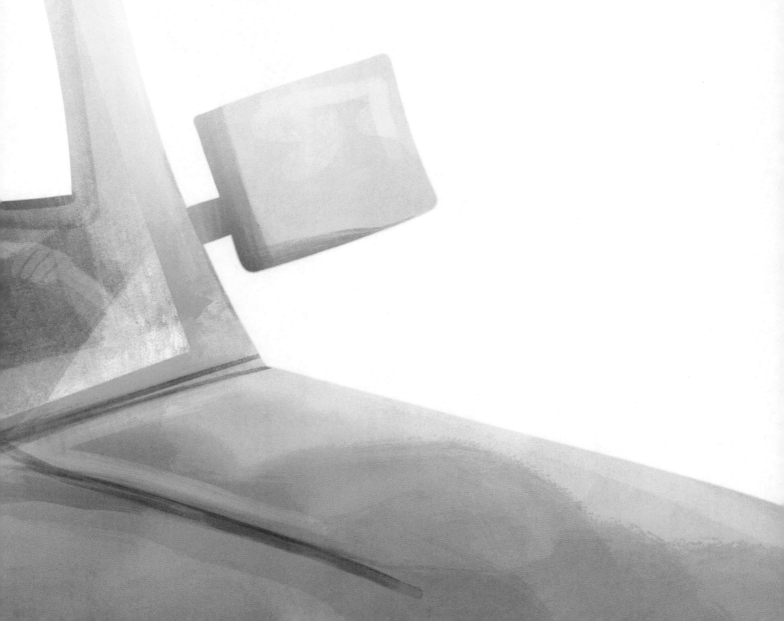

At the pool, Negative Ned's voice pops into Sticky Icky Vicky's head.

"Why try, when you are going to fail? Go get icky and sticky instead."

"Not today," Vicky replies, as she watches Betty and Rhea jump into the pool.

Wanting to join them, but still too scared to jump in, Vicky feels like a fool.

She stares at the calm pool water and starts to feel hot and sweaty.
"You can do this, Sticky Icky Vicky, you are brave and tough," says Betty.
But all Vicky hears are loud ocean waves as she shudders with fear.
"You can't do it! Remember the rogue wave," Negative Ned says with a jeer.
Determined to overcome her fear, Vicky chooses to ignore Negative Ned.
She decides to stop listening to the negative thoughts in her head.

"Come on Sticky Icky Vicky," says Rhea with a smile, "get into the pool!"
Vicky slowly wades knee-deep into the water, now feeling calm and cool.
She plucks up the courage, bends over, and splashes water onto her face,
the sound of ocean waves disappearing as she feels the water's warm embrace.
Betty calls from the deep end of the pool, "Sticky Icky Vicky, come over here!"
Vicky courageously wades deeper into the pool, showing no sign of fear.

She then dunks her head under the water and blows out big bubbles.

As Vicky blows the bubbles, she blows away her fear and water troubles.

When she finally climbs out of the pool, she gives an excited **SQUEAL OF DELIGHT.**

"Betty," Vicky shouts, "there is nothing to keep me from your party in a fortnight!"

At Betty's birthday party, Sticky Icky Vicky is having so much fun.
She is drenched from head to toe, playing on the splash pad with everyone.
Rhea and Vicky ride down waterslides, screaming happily for all to hear.
"Look what you could have missed," says Rhea, "if you still had your water fear."
"I know," Vicky replies, smiling as she climbs the stairs to the next waterslide.
"It was not easy, but I had the courage and belief in myself," she says with pride.

Vicky's courage sparks a new voice in her head.

She calls this helpful inner voice, Positive Ted.

Positive Ted tells Vicky that she is good enough.

He also reminds her that she can be brave and tough.

"If you fail or make mistakes," says Ted, "it is a great thing,

because you learn from them and get better at anything!"

Vicky has a heart full of courage, now she listens to Ted's positive voice.

She has learnt to work hard to get what she wants, because she has that choice.

"With effort," says Ted, "you will learn and get to do some amazing things."
Vicky is now braver, enjoying all the adventures that life brings.
"When I do my best," Vicky says, "I know I can't go wrong.
This is why I'm no longer afraid to face any fears that come along!"

Vicky still loves getting all icky and sticky, but this is not where the fun ends.
She also goes swimming in the ocean and jumps in the waves with her friends.

Vicky has learnt to snorkel and surf and now bathes every day of the year.
She always listens to her helpful inner voice and chooses COURAGE OVER FEAR.

Your choices and who you listen to will decide how you act and feel in every way.
Always **BELIEVE IN YOURSELF** and work towards doing your best, starting from today.

Use the statements and questions below to start having a conversation about fear:

Fear is a feeling of being afraid.
Everyone experiences fear and it is ok to have these feelings. Just don't let the fear stop you from doing things you like, love or need to do.

Do you know of any situation that has made you fearful to do something you like, love or need to do?

Who can you talk to about your fear and how to overcome it?

You can talk about your fear with friends and family, and they can help you build the courage to take steps towards overcoming it

Once you have faced your fear and overcome it, how do you think you will feel?

What was a situation where you felt scared and are now brave?

How do you think you could help yourself and others to face their fears?

What do you think will happen if you don't get the courage to get past this fear?

Do you have any negative thoughts about yourself? What are they?

Do you have any positive thoughts about yourself? What are they?

ABOUT THE AUTHORS

Michael and Alysia are husband and wife health professionals who live in the Australian capital, Canberra, with their children, a dog, an African grey parrot, two turtles and some chickens.

In 2019, they decided to write a book that inspired children to believe that, no matter what, they had the power to choose to overcome their fears. The consequences of the choices we make will shape our behaviour and shape our lives into what we will become.

ABOUT THE ILLUSTRATOR

Noor Alshalabi is a Jordan-based illustrator who started drawing ever since she learnt how to hold a pencil.

After getting her BA in Visual Arts and Design, she pursued her dream of turning her imagination into reality through children's books.
You can always find her with a cup of coffee, curled up with a good book, watching movies, playing with her pet bird, spending time with a friend, or going for a hike. Nature is both her source of inspiration and relaxation.

LISTEN TO THIS BOOK!

Read along by either scanning the QR code or use the link provided for a free audio reading of this book.

http://bit.ly/Vickysaudiobook

For any questions or to tell us what you think of the story, email us at
hello@stickyickyvicky.com

If you want to learn more about Sticky Icky Vicky and her journey, go to
www.stickyickyvicky.com